TRAMPY'S BIRTHDAY SURPRISE

by James Driscoll
Illustrated by Rob Lee

Storm Publishing

It was a lovely summer's day. The flowers looked at their very best. They were all showing off their beautiful colours. There was a very slight breeze that made the flowers swing to and fro. They looked as though they were dancing. The song of a skylark could be heard in the distance.

The Shoe People decided that this was the perfect day for a walk in the country.

They were discussing what they should take, when P.C. Boot, who was looking through his notebook, looked up and said,

"Well this time we really have done it. Here it is in my notebook, as plain as plain, in black and white, written by my hand, signed and dated . . ."

"For goodness sake P.C. Boot what have we done?" asked Charlie.

"Done? What have we done?" he asked. "Forgotten Trampy's birthday, that's all," said P.C. Boot, shaking his head.

"Poor Trampy. So that's why he looked so sad this morning," said Margot.

P.C. Boot pushed his helmet back on his head and put his hand on his forehead.

"Something has to be done, let me think, let me think," he said. "I know what we'll do. Trampy loves the countryside. When he comes back we will ask him to come for a walk with us. We won't tell him that we know that it's his birthday. We'll pack the picnic basket and give him a lovely birthday party in the country."

"What a brilliant idea, I will perform some of my funniest tricks and make him laugh," said Charlie.

They began to pack the picnic basket.

Charlie was very busy looking in his big trick box. He found a very large spring which he closed and placed under his hat. He took out lots of coloured handkerchiefs and pushed them into his pockets. He filled the daisy on the top of his hat with water.

Margot had just finished putting the cakes into the picnic basket when she heard Trampy coming. She quickly closed the lid and fastened the basket so that he wouldn't see what was inside.

"Hello Trampy. We are going for a walk in the country. Margot has put a few things in the picnic basket. Do you want to come with us?" asked P.C. Boot.

"No thank you Constable Boot, I don't feel at my best today," said Trampy in a very sad voice.

"Please come Trampy," pleaded Margot holding his hand. "We always have such fun with you. Please Trampy, just for me, I will be so unhappy if you don't come."

"Dear Margot, how could I possibly make you unhappy? Of course I'll come," replied Trampy and they all set off for the countryside.

"That looks a very good field to have our picnic in," said P.C. Boot pointing to a field with lots of small bales of hay.

P.C. Boot and Charlie carried the picnic basket into the field and placed it down very carefully. Margot spread a very large blue and white checked tablecloth over the grass and began to place the lovely party food on to it. There were little fancy cakes, a very big creamy trifle, a red jelly and a green jelly and lots of sweets. There was also a large jug of delicious orange juice.

Trampy, Charlie and P.C. Boot were at the far side of the field.

"This is marvellous," said Charlie pointing to six bales of hay which had been placed in a circle. "I can use these for my performance. They look just like a circus ring. You can all sit on them and have ringside seats."

Trampy called Margot to come and watch Charlie's circus act.

Margot, Trampy and P.C. Boot sat waiting for the show to begin. There was a loud clash of cymbals and suddenly Charlie somersaulted off the top of one of the bales of hay right into the centre of the ring.

They all clapped and cheered.

"Ladies and Gentlemen, today is a very special day," said Charlie. "And this show is a special birthday surprise for our dear friend Trampy. We want to wish you the happiest of happy birthdays."

With that he released the spring under his hat sending it high into the sky. He then pulled silly faces and made his hair stand on end. As his bowler hat fell through the air back to the ground, Charlie flicked the brim of the hat with his toecap. The hat turned over and over in the air and then landed straight back on his head. Margot, Trampy and P.C. Boot laughed so much that it made their tummies hurt.

"Happy Birthday, Trampy!" cried Charlie taking a final bow and squirting water from the daisy on his hat.

Margot and P.C. Boot clapped and clapped. Trampy gave his loudest whistle.

They returned to where the picnic had been placed. Margot reached into the picnic basket and took out a lovely birthday cake covered in delicious icing. There was one red candle on the top. She placed the cake in the middle of the tablecloth and P.C. Boot lit the candle.

They all sang happy birthday to Trampy.

Trampy blew out the candle. They all cheered.

"Thank you so much. This has been the best party I have ever had and I thought you had all forgotten my birthday," said Trampy.

P.C. Boot looked at Margot and Charlie and winked.